Henry lofted the ball toward the goal, right in front of Clayton.

The goalie made his move, straight toward the ball, but Clayton got there first. He leaped and trapped the ball on his chest and dropped it at his feet. He faked to his right and then broke to the left.

The goalie took the fake for just an instant, and it gave Clayton the room he needed.

Bam!

Books about the kids from Angel Park:

Angel Park All-Stars

Angel Park Soccer Stars

KICKOFF TIME

By Dean Hughes

Illustrated by Dennis Lyall

Bullseye Books • Alfred A. Knopf
New York

A BULLSEYE BOOK PUBLISHED BY ALFRED A. KNOPF, INC.
Copyright © 1991 by Dean Hughes
Cover art copyright © 1991 by Rick Ormond
Interior illustrations copyright © 1991 by Dennis Lyall
ANGEL PARK ALL-STARS characters copyright © 1989
by Alfred A. Knopf, Inc.
ANGEL PARK SOCCER STARS characters copyright © 1991
by Alfred A. Knopf, Inc.

Library of Congress Cataloging-in-Publication Data
Hughes, Dean, 1943–
Kickoff time / by Dean Hughes ; illustrated by Dennis Lyall.
p.   cm. — (Angel Park soccer stars ; 1)
Summary: Jacob Scott, of Angel Park baseball fame, finds out first-
hand that soccer is just as exciting as baseball, and maybe more
demanding.
ISBN 0-679-81542-2 (pbk.) — ISBN 0-679-91542-7 (lib. bdg.)
[1. Soccer—Fiction.]   I. Lyall, Dennis, ill.   II. Title.
III. Series: Hughes, Dean, 1943– Angel Park soccer stars ; 1
PZ7.H87312Ki   1991   [Fic]—dc20   91-10601
RL: 4.4
First Bullseye Books edition: October 1991

Manufactured in the United States of America
10   9   8   7   6   5   4   3   2

for McKay Matheson

★1★

Getting Together

===

Jacob Scott closed in on the boy with the ball. He tried to remember what his coach had told him about defense.

Stay balanced.

Watch the ball, not the player's body movements.

This time Jacob was going to steal the ball. Clayton Lindsay, the English kid, had made him look bad a couple of times already.

And then Clayton made a mistake.

He stopped the ball out in front. Jacob saw his chance and swiped at it with his right foot.

But the ball wasn't there!

Somehow Clayton had flicked it away. And

with Jacob's balance off, Clayton broke past him and was *gone*!

As he charged by, Jacob heard him laugh.

"No, no, no, Jacob," Coach Toscano said. "He tricked you. He put the ball there to dare you. But you were too far back. You have to move in tight before you tackle."

Then he showed Jacob. He came in close with his body, blocking his shoulders against Jacob's. He stayed square to him and never let his balance swing too far to either side.

Jacob understood. But he wished the word "tackle" in soccer meant what it did to American football players. He would like to grab Clayton and bring him down.

And now the guy was showing off again.

While the coach was helping Jacob, Clayton started juggling. He kept the ball in the air, bouncing it off his feet and his thighs. He was a big kid for a sixth grader, and he looked old. He even talked as though he were more grown up than the rest. He wore his hair quite long, and he had a way of cocking his head back when he talked.

Coach Toscano finally looked over and said, "Good juggling, Clayton, but let's concentrate on our drills."

The coach was Brazilian, but he had been in the United States since he was a teenager, so he didn't have much of an accent. Jacob liked him. The coach had fun with the boys and laughed a lot, but he knew his soccer, inside and out. And he knew how to teach it.

He could play the game too. He looked like Pelé, the great Brazilian player—muscular legs and compact body, and *quick.*

This was the first day of practice, and so far the coach had been working on basic skills. Jacob needed that. He had played the year before in the recreation league in his little town of Angel Park, California. And he had done all right.

But Coach Toscano had invited him to play on a competition team. It was an "under twelve" league, but most of these kids had played a lot. Jacob was sure he was the worst player there.

"Clayton's good, isn't he?" Nate Matheson said to Jacob. Jacob knew Nate from school. The guy was a soccer *nut.* Soccer was about the only thing he ever talked about.

"Yeah, but he acts like a hotshot."

"Not really," Nate said. "He's okay. I'd

probably show off too if I could juggle like that."

"I thought *you* were the best player on the team."

Nate laughed. He was a tall kid with hair so blond it was almost white—and it was always a mess, even though he wore a sweatband to hold it down. "I'm a pretty good goalie, but I can't control the ball like Clayton. He's grown up with soccer. His dad was a club player in England."

"What's a club player?"

"You don't know much about soccer, do you?"

"I guess not."

"Club players are pros. It's like making the majors in baseball over here."

"Do they get paid much?"

"Are you kidding?" Nate rolled his eyes. "Soccer players are some of the highest paid athletes in the *world*. More people play soccer—it's really called *football* everywhere but here—than any other sport. And more people go to soccer games. During World Cup, more people—"

"Okay. Okay. I know you *love* soccer," Jacob said.

"Don't you?"

Jacob shrugged. "It's okay."

Nate looked disgusted. "Why play if you don't like it?"

Jacob really didn't want to get into this. "It's fun," he finally said. "But I'm a baseball player."

"Hey, this is competition league, Jacob. We're *serious*."

"I know. I'll play hard. It's just not my favorite sport."

The truth was, Jacob had wanted to play basketball with his friends Kenny and Harlan. But he was short, and he probably always would be. That's why his mom—a PE teacher—told him to try soccer. She said it would make him a better baseball player.

Heidi Wells was standing nearby. She was good friends with Nate. The two had played soccer together since they were little kids. "Jacob, we want to be *good* this year," she said.

But she didn't finish what she had started to say. The coach called everyone over. He had the players work in teams of six—three on three, attackers and defenders. The attacking team worked on crisp, accurate passes, and the defenders tried to take the ball.

Jacob found it hard. The coach assigned Heidi to guard Jacob (except he called it "marking," not guarding), and she kept taking the ball away from him before he could pass it off.

She had dark hair, cut short, and a wide, square-cornered sort of smile. She laughed a lot too. But on the soccer field, she was all business. She had long runner's legs, and she was quick. Jacob couldn't shake her loose, and he was very fast.

The coach seemed to take more time with Jacob than anyone else. "Make a quick decision," he told Jacob. "Pass before she marks you so close. As soon as you pass, break to open space."

And then, when Jacob did a better job, Coach Toscano laughed and shouted, "Yes, yes. Wonderful. Much better!"

That felt good. Jacob did think he was getting the idea.

When practice was over, Heidi told Jacob, "You catch on to things quick. You're going to be good."

Jacob liked her. As good as she was, she didn't have to compliment Jacob. "I wish I could play the way you do," he told her.

"Well, sure," she said with a serious look. "But the whole world wishes that." And then that funny, square-cornered smile appeared, and she started to laugh.

"I'll tell you what," Jacob said. "I'll forget about baseball for now. I'll give soccer my best shot."

"Good!" she said. "Do it, Jacob! Some day they'll build a statue of you in this town. Nate and I already have spots picked out for our statues. Nate's is down by the city dump."

She burst out laughing and then walked away.

Jacob thought she was sort of weird.

He also liked her.

Before Jacob left, he talked to his friends from the baseball team: Henry White, Sterling Malone, Billy Bacon, and Lian Jie. They had all been on the competition soccer team the year before.

Henry was not the sort of guy who had to have a lot of attention. Whatever position the coach asked him to play, he would play well. And he had the quickness and athletic ability to make good things happen.

Sterling was big and strong, but he was also fast. The year before he had been one of the best fullbacks in the league because he was such a powerhouse on defense.

And Billy Bacon wasn't bad either. He didn't have much speed, but he was strong, and a good defensive player.

Lian Jie, who was Taiwanese, hadn't played much soccer, but he was a natural athlete, and he was picking up the skills fast.

"It's a good sport," Sterling told Jacob. "In some ways, I like it better than baseball."

Jacob was surprised. But it was something to think about.

He did know that he liked a lot of the players—and some of them were really good athletes. One guy named Chris Baca could dribble and shoot almost as well as Clayton. He was a quiet guy, but he was built solid, and he turned fierce on the soccer field.

A girl named Tammy Hill had done a great job on defense. And that didn't surprise Jacob a bit. She was good at all sports. She was small, but she was a gymnast, and she had great body control.

Another player Jacob knew from school, Brian Rohatinsky, came up to him and said, "I didn't know you were so fast, Jacob."

During drills Brian had stolen the ball more than anyone. Jacob had been surprised. Brian was a brainy kid in school, and Jacob hadn't thought of him as an athlete. He wore goggles on the field in place of the glasses he wore at school. He looked sort of strange, but the guy could play.

"I've got a lot to learn," Jacob said.

Just then Clayton walked by. "Sorry to have faked you out so badly," he said. "But it was a good lesson for you."

Jacob didn't say anything to Clayton, but he made a promise to himself. Before the season was over, he would show Clayton he could play this game.

As Jacob was leaving, Coach Toscano stopped him and said, "Jacob, you have what it takes to be a *great* soccer player. You're quick and agile. And you listen to what I tell you."

"I'm the worst player on the team," Jacob said.

"Yes, you are," the coach said, and that flashing grin of his spread across his face. "I'm glad you know that."

Jacob was taken by surprise.

"But you're working hard to catch up. And you can do it. You have less experience than anyone—except for Lian—but if you work hard enough, you can be one of our best."

Jacob liked hearing that. And he made up his mind he was going to play the game well. Baseball would always be his first love, but he liked soccer.

When he got home, his mom asked him how things had gone. "Great," Jacob said. "I think we're going to have a good team."

"I thought you didn't like soccer."

"It's okay."

"Just something to do in the fall, after baseball?"

Jacob grinned, showing the split between his front teeth. He was a freckle-faced boy who looked sort of young for his age, but his deep voice sounded surprisingly grown up.

He held his fist to his mouth, as though it were a microphone, and pretended to be a radio announcer. "Jacob Scott, the star right fielder, is now playing soccer in the off-season. What do you think of that, Hank?"

His voice took on a western twang as he answered himself. "Well, Frank, I'd say that Jacob Scott is one of the truly great athletes of our time."

Mrs. Scott shook her head and laughed. And then she said, "What did I start this time?"

★ 2 ★

Practice Game

===================

The Angel Park soccer team practiced almost every day for the next two weeks. Jacob had never worked so hard in his life. Baseball practices had been a piece of cake compared to this.

Soccer practice meant *running*. The coach said that the team that was in shape was the one that would come through in close games. And that meant *work*.

Jacob was learning fast. His techniques for moving the ball upfield with his feet—what soccer players call "dribbling"—were weak. But he was becoming a better defender, and his passing was improving.

Still, Jacob knew he had a long way to go. The coach arranged a practice game at the end of the second week. And that's when he surprised Jacob.

He had everyone sit on the grass. They were wearing their game uniforms—white shorts and a blue shirt—for the first time. Jacob was excited. He hoped he might get some playing time.

But then Coach Toscano read the starting lineup:

Goalkeeper	Nate Matheson
Left forward	Clayton Lindsay
Right forward	Heidi Wells
Left wing	Chris Baca
Right wing	Henry White
Fullbacks	Jared Trajillo
	Tammy Hill
	Sterling Malone
Sweeper	Brian Rohatinsky

It all sounded about the way Jacob had expected, but then the coach said, "I'm going to try Lian Jie and Jacob Scott at midfield. They're inexperienced, but they're fast, and they both have the potential to play the position well."

Jacob felt about two seconds of joy, and then it hit him. He was going to be starting, and he wasn't good enough. He was going to look like an idiot out there!

The coach added, "Adam Snarr, you'll play at wing when you go in the game. Tanya Gardner, midfield or wing. Billy Bacon, fullback. Trenton Daynes, fullback or sweeper."

Jacob was hardly listening. Why would the coach do this?

Coach Toscano seemed to know what Jacob was thinking. As the players headed for the field, he walked over and put his hand on Jacob's shoulder. "Jacob, you've worked harder than anyone in practice. But you'll learn more in a game. That's why I want you out there."

Jacob wasn't quite sure how to take that. Maybe he had earned a starting position, or maybe the coach just knew he needed experience. Either way, Jacob was scared.

"Blue Springs has a player named Jackson—number eleven," the coach said. "He's *very* fast and *very* good. I want you to mark him. You're fast enough to stay with him."

Jacob felt sort of sick. "Coach, Henry's

really fast, and so is Chris. Maybe they could do better than—"

"No. I want them on the wings. Sterling is fast, too, but I need some speed at fullback. I want you in the middle." And then he laughed. "Jackson will teach you some things," he said.

Jacob didn't like the sound of that.

When the teams lined up for the kickoff, Jacob wasn't sure where he was supposed to go. Sterling pointed to his position, and then he yelled, "Good luck with Robbie Jackson. Just stay after him the best you can. He'll be all over you."

He made the kid sound like a rash.

"I'll try," Jacob said, but not loud enough for anyone to hear.

He jumped up and down a few times to stay warmed-up. But he thought he would explode before the referee finally set the ball down for the kickoff. Not many parents had come to the game—since it was only for practice—but Jacob's parents were there.

His mom waved, and she looked pleased that Jacob was starting. But she had no idea how scared Jacob was.

Finally the Blue Springs Springers put the

ball in play, and Jacob marked his man. He stayed right on him. The left wing kept looking his way, and Jacob knew that he wanted to get the ball to Jackson, but Jacob marked him tight.

And then, when the wing tried to dribble past Sterling, Sterling moved in with a solid tackle and kicked the ball loose.

Tammy Hill came up and made a good trap, and just like that, Angel Park had the ball and was on the attack.

Maybe this Jackson kid wasn't all *that* great. Jacob could stay with him.

Tammy passed quickly to Chris Baca on the wing, and he started dribbling up the sideline—what soccer players call the "touchline."

But Chris was cut off there, and Jacob saw he needed help. He made a sudden feint to his right, and then darted to his left. He was open, a good two steps ahead of Jackson, and Chris turned and fired a strong pass.

Jacob trapped the ball with the inside of his foot, and then broke forward, trying to dribble. But in his hurry he had lost track of where his teammates were, and now Jackson had caught up.

Jacob slowed. He was suddenly desperate. He glanced quickly to his left, saw Heidi coming up, and tried to pass off.

But the ball was gone!

Jackson had made a quick slide tackle and had knocked the ball toward the center of the field. A Blue Springs fullback controlled it and then passed to a midfielder. Jacob raced after him, but Lian yelled, "I've got him. Get your own man."

It was too late. By the time he could stop and reverse himself, Jackson was breaking up the field—*fast*. He took a sharp pass from the other midfielder.

When Jacob finally caught up with him, Jackson kicked the ball to a forward, who was breaking toward the goal.

Jared Trajillo, one of the Angel Park fullbacks, picked up the forward, but too late again. The forward chipped the ball to the Blue Springs inside forward, Peter Metzger. He was a German kid, and everyone said he was *good*.

Metzger took the pass in the air and smashed a strong volley shot at the corner of the goal.

Nate dove, but he had no chance.

Only luck saved Angel Park.

The shot was wide, and it bounced off the goalpost.

The Blue Springs wing tried to get a shot off the rebound, but Brian Rohatinsky, the Angel Park sweeper, got to the ball first and passed it back to Nate. Nate cleared the ball with a long punt upfield.

But Jacob knew he had dodged a bullet, so to speak. He had lost the ball, and then he had gotten beat by the man he was supposed to mark.

This was tough. He was already out of breath.

But he had no time to think about that. A Blue Springs player "headed" the long punt back toward his own right wing, and the Springers were already on the attack again.

Jacob marked Jackson closely this time, but the guy was *quick*. He blasted up the field, and Jacob ran all out to stay with him. But then Jackson stopped suddenly.

The wing hit Jackson with a pass just as Jacob overran him.

Jacob recovered and marked Jackson again.

For a moment, the two stood face to face, and then Jackson passed off to—

No, he faked!

And Jacob took the fake.

Suddenly the guy was gone, dribbling past Jacob. He shot a long pass upfield to Metzger. Metzger put a fake on Sterling and broke into the open.

And then it was Metzger against Nate, and Nate didn't have a chance. Metzger drove forward, and Nate came out to meet him. But Metzger powered a shot into the bottom right corner of the net.

Goal!

The score was 1 to 0.

Jacob stopped and put his hands on his knees. He couldn't believe he could be *this* tired so soon.

And that wasn't the worst. He didn't think he could cover Jackson. The guy was just too good.

"That's all right, Jacob," the coach yelled. "That's how you learn." But then the coach yelled, "Where were you, Brian? You have to back up your fullbacks."

Jacob wasn't even sure which player did what out there. The only thing he knew for sure was that he was stinking up the whole place, and he was embarrassed.

But he had no time to feel sorry for himself. Angel Park was kicking off again, and Jacob had to try and stay open—which meant staying free of Jackson.

But it was too late! Blue Springs had already stolen the ball—and before Jacob knew it, Jackson had taken a pass from a wing and was dribbling straight toward Jacob.

And now Jackson seemed to know he was facing a kid he could handle. He looked up at Jacob with a smile on his face.

Jacob got ready.

He let Jackson move in on him. He stayed on the balls of his feet the way the coach had taught him. And he kept himself square so he could break in either direction when Jackson made his move.

But Jackson was walking with the ball, taking his time as though he were tired. He even faked a yawn. Jacob took this chance to move in tighter.

He wanted that ball. And he wanted to show this guy that he was no pushover. He watched the ball, waited for his chance, and then he took a sweeping kick at it.

But just as he started his foot forward, Jackson seemed to spot what he was waiting for. He caught Jacob off balance, and he flicked the ball to his left. Then he shot past Jacob, picked the ball back up, and was gone.

He charged ahead as Jacob raced to catch up, and then he passed off to a wing, broke toward the goal, and got a quick pass back.

Sterling picked Jackson up and stopped his charge. And Tammy Hill came in and stole the ball.

So at least Jackson didn't score. But no thanks to Jacob!

Jacob knew he had to do better. He got on Jackson again and tried to cover his every move.

But Jackson never stopped changing directions, faking, running. And once he got the ball, he either passed off quickly, or he used feints to keep Jacob off balance.

Then, when Jacob got the ball on attack, Jackson was in his face.

Jacob tried to use some of Jackson's techniques. But when he looked around to pass, Jackson would move in for a tackle. Dribbling was even worse. Jacob just didn't have the skill to deceive this guy.

After a time, Jacob didn't want to get the ball. And on defense, every time he thought he knew how to stop his man, Jackson would do something different.

"Look out! Look out! Here I come," Jackson would grunt at Jacob, and then he would bark "Gotcha!" when he broke by him.

Time and again the Blue Springs team got the ball into shooting position, and Metzger got off good shots. The fullbacks started doubling him, but that only opened the other striker, and he got off good shots too.

Nate played well and stopped most of the shots. But when halftime came, the score was 3 to 0.

The Angel Park players walked off the field with their heads down. They looked as though they had already lost the game.

Clayton had his hands on his hips as he walked by Jacob. He brushed back his long brown hair with his fingers. "A bit over-matched, aren't you?" he said, and he sounded angry.

"I'm doing my best," Jacob said.

"Well, it isn't good enough."

Jerk, Jacob thought. But he also knew that Clayton was right.

★ 3 ★

Signs of Life

At halftime, as the players sat on the grass beyond one of the goal lines, Coach Toscano seemed as happy as if the team were *ahead* 3 to 0. Jacob couldn't figure him out.

"Hey, kids, you're learning. The defense keeps getting better. Now we have to get after them. We have to move on to the attack."

But that's when Clayton exploded. "Attack?" he yelled. "We don't have any attack! I hardly touched the ball. These guys we have playing midfield lose the ball every time they touch it."

"Clayton, I'll hear none of that kind of talk," the coach answered. "We're a team."

"I know, but if they can't—"

"Clayton, no more. Talk that way again and you won't be on our team. We're going to be good—*very* good—but we can't get that way overnight. We all have a lot to learn."

Clayton looked ready to speak again—then seemed to think better of it.

The coach wasn't finished. "A soccer team isn't a bunch of parts. It's *one thing*. In some sports you can get by with lots of talented individuals. But a soccer team has to fit together perfectly. Do you understand that?"

Clayton didn't answer. He flopped on his back in the grass.

Jacob couldn't really blame Clayton for being upset. He knew how he would feel if a new guy on the baseball team had gotten to start but then kept messing up.

But Sterling Malone leaned over and said, "Clayton loses his temper sometimes. But he doesn't really mean all that stuff."

"He's right, though," Jacob said. "I can't stay with Jackson."

"Who can?" Sterling said. "Did you see

him smoke me? *Whoosh!*" He motioned with his thumb past his shoulder. Sterling was a big guy, but he was so fast that not many players got past him. But Jackson had. At least Sterling could admit that, even if Clayton couldn't. But then, maybe no one ever blew past Clayton.

Coach Toscano told the players they could all go get a drink of water before the second half started. But the players got up slowly and walked to the fountain. They seemed tired.

"Jacob," Heidi said as she came up behind him. "Jackson keeps getting by you because you're watching his fakes. Remember what the coach always says. Keep your eye on the ball."

Jacob nodded. "Okay," he said. "I do try to remember that, but it's hard."

"Hey, I know. We all make that mistake. That's why the coach keeps repeating it."

Nate walked over to them. "Jacob, don't let Clayton bother you," he said. "Jackson is good. But there are eleven of us out there. One player can't stop someone like that."

"That's right," Heidi said. "Cut him off

and slow him down. That gives the rest of us time to help. You're probably better off if you don't even try to steal the ball. Just keep him from breaking loose—so he has to pass off."

Jacob said he would do that. And he felt better. Nate and Heidi were good friends already. And Sterling was a good guy. That made this whole thing easier.

As it turned out, however, the coach had Adam Snarr start the second half in place of Jacob. And Jacob could see that Adam was a better player.

Adam was about Jacob's size—very small— but on attack he knew how to get his body between himself and the defender. His voice was funny, sort of squeaky, but he used it to let his teammates know where he was.

Still, Blue Springs kept the pressure on. A few minutes into the second half, the girl playing right wing centered a pass in front of the goal. Metzger jumped above everyone else and headed the ball at the goal.

Nate made a good block, but the ball bounced loose, and Metzger picked it back up. He made a quick move to the left and took the defense with him. And then, just as quickly, he cut back to the right.

He was only ahead of Jared by half a step, but he saw his chance and slapped a hard shot right past Nate's feet.

The ball got by Nate before he could react in time.

And now the score was 4 to 0.

Jackson wasn't the only great player on this team. Jacob wondered whether his team would ever start looking like they belonged on the same field with these kids.

"Give him more help," the coach was yelling. "You fullbacks have to get up in the air with the forward. And you have to watch for those rebounds. Someone should have gotten on that ball."

Jacob could see all that. But he didn't think they had anyone who could jump as high—or who could react as quickly. He really wondered if Angel Park would get killed in every game all season.

But halfway through the second half, the coach sent Jacob back in, this time for Lian. Jacob was now marking the other midfielder, and the guy wasn't nearly as quick as Jackson. This kid worked and worked, but he couldn't get free of Jacob.

Jackson tried a pass to him once, and Jacob cut it off. The next time Jackson got the ball, he kept it, and he tried to dribble up the middle.

He did get a step ahead of Adam, but Tammy Hill came up to help. She was small but really agile, and she wasn't afraid to take Jackson on. She and Adam doubled him, and then Tammy stepped in and knocked the ball away.

She chased it down and controlled it, and then she flicked it out to Billy, who was now playing fullback. Billy passed quickly up to Jacob.

Jacob had learned his lesson about dribbling against Jackson. He spotted Adam breaking away from his defender, and he smacked a quick instep pass. He tried to lead Adam, and the pass was a little long, but Adam ran it down.

Then Adam dribbled a few yards up the field as Jacob broke past his defender to take the return pass. He was open, so he took the ball with him on a short run. Then he flipped it off the outside of his foot to Sterling on the wing.

Sterling made a quick move up the touchline, then stopped, faked, and broke on an angle toward the goal. He had his man beat, but a fullback came up to meet him.

That left Clayton open.

Sterling lofted the ball toward the goal, right in front of Clayton.

The goalie made his move, straight toward the ball, but Clayton got there first. He leaped and trapped the ball on his chest and dropped it at his feet. He faked to his right and then broke to the left.

The goalie took the fake for just an instant, and it gave Clayton the room he needed.

Bam!

Clayton's right foot swung like a whip, and the ball snapped into the net.

Clayton leaped straight in the air, and then most of the Angel Park players mobbed him.

They were down 4 to 1, and no one really thought they had a chance to win. But they had scored. And they had worked the ball well. They had actually looked like a real soccer team!

Jacob stayed back while the other players celebrated.

He didn't really feel like part of the team yet. And he knew what Clayton thought of him.

Still, Jacob knew he was playing better. He had made a couple of pretty good passes, and he was marking his man well. He had learned a lot today. And he had made up his mind that he was going to work harder than ever to learn the skills that he now knew he needed.

Jacob felt even better when Angel Park scored again, even if he hadn't been exactly in on the play. He knew he was making things tough in the middle for Blue Springs, and that was giving his team the ball more often.

But just when it seemed they might actually have a shot at winning, Blue Springs broke away, and the girl who played their right wing took a pass from that hotshot Metzger and drove the ball home.

And only a couple of minutes later, they scored again.

Blue Springs ended up winning 6 to 2.

When the game was over, the Angel Park players dragged themselves off the field. They looked tired, but even more, they looked *beaten.*

"Okay. *Excellent!*" Coach Toscano told them. "Now you know what it's going to take. Those kids were more fit than you were. That means we have to work harder. And we have to sharpen our skills."

Some of the kids groaned. But the coach only laughed. "I'll tell you what," he said. "We have *talent.* We have more of it than Blue Springs. They have two very good players. We have a *team* of good athletes. We'll beat them some time this year."

But no one cheered. Everyone was too tired.

"Oh, one more thing. What are we going to call this team? We have to think of a name."

"How about the Tortoises?" Heidi said.

"Oh, no. Something *fast!*"

"Lizards?" Billy Bacon yelled out.

"No, no. Something better looking than a lizard."

"Hey, I like lizards," Billy said. "They're fun to scare girls with."

"They don't scare me," Tammy said.

Tanya Gardner said, "Me neither." She hadn't played in the game much today, and Jacob wondered if she was mad about that. She was probably a better player than he was. But she seemed to be in a pretty good mood.

"No, no. No lizards," the coach said. "They scare *me*."

All the kids laughed, and Clayton said, "Well, then, that might be just the thing."

Jacob was surprised that Clayton could sound so happy. Maybe he wasn't such a bad guy. But he sure wasn't apologizing for what he had said at halftime.

The coach said he would not have a team named the Lizards, but no one could come up with anything better. So the team still didn't have a name when the players left.

Jacob stumbled over to his parents. "I'm *shot*," he said.

"So what do you think of soccer now?" his mother asked, and she laughed.

"We didn't run this hard last year," Jacob said. "No one was as fast as that Jackson kid."

"You're fast too," she said, and she patted him on the back.

"Fast enough for baseball. But I don't know if I've got enough speed for this game—or if I'll ever be able to *play* the game."

"Come on, now," his dad said, but he didn't know anything about sports.

His mom, on the other hand, taught PE. "Remember how much more time you've put into baseball," she said. "You can be good at soccer if you want to be."

"Okay, coach," Jacob said, and he grinned.

His mom laughed, but Nate was yelling at Jacob. "Can you meet me and Heidi after school tomorrow? We can help you work on some of your skills."

Jacob shouted back, "Yeah, I'll be there. If I can walk."

"You won't have to walk," Heidi yelled. "We'll be running the whole time."

Jacob groaned. What a game!

Practice Makes . . . Tired Legs

Jacob met Nate and Heidi after school the next day. The soccer fields were in the same park where Jacob played baseball. Angel Park had always had great baseball teams, and big crowds even came to the Little League games. But soccer was just starting to become popular.

All the same, Jacob sort of wished he had a glove and bat with him instead of his soccer cleats. He didn't say that to his friends, however.

It was a hot day even though it was October. Angel Park was in desert country, and the weather stayed warm most of the year. That was nice for sports, but Jacob was still dragging from the day before. He could have used a little cool air.

But Nate and Heidi didn't seem tired. They were doing some juggling to "warm up." Jacob stopped and watched, but then Heidi said, while she was still juggling, "You need to practice this, Jacob. You don't even have a ball, do you?"

"Uh, no."

And then Nate said, "Jacob, you should *live* with a soccer ball. You can practice against a wall, or against your garage, and you can juggle." He grunted as he reached to kick the ball into the air and then catch it with his thigh. "You should be spending every spare minute doing this."

"Yeah. Then I could be a juggler when I grow up."

The ball got away from Nate, and he ran after it. But as he walked back, he said, "Jacob, you have to get so the ball seems like part of you."

"Yeah, right." Jacob had heard the coach say that twenty times already. But he couldn't imagine it.

"Yeah," Heidi said. "You should sleep with

a soccer ball in your arms—and give it a great big kiss good night. That's what Nate does. Of course, I take my ball out for a walk every afternoon. And sometimes we play 'fetch' together. Come here, ball. Bring me the ball, ball."

"You're really strange, Heidi," Jacob said. "*Really* strange."

Heidi burst out laughing, the way she always did, but as soon as the three started to practice, she got serious. She and Nate showed Jacob some of the mistakes he had made in the game.

And Jacob knew exactly what was happening. Nate and Heidi had made him a "project." They wanted the team to be good, and that meant Jacob had to improve.

Heidi was a good passer and shooter, and she showed Jacob that he was sometimes striking the ball wrong. Most passes needed to be low and fast. The snap came from the lower leg—from the knee down—not from long, wild kicks.

She had Nate mark him, and then Jacob tried to make swift, accurate passes to Heidi as she broke in one direction or another.

But shooting was a little different. She showed him how to get power kicks off his shoelaces. His shots were sailing high until she had him lean forward over the ball.

"Land on the same foot you kick with," she told him. "That keeps your weight forward."

And it worked.

After a time, Jacob was driving his shots low and hard, and he was getting them past Nate.

That was exciting.

"Better. A lot better," Nate yelled. "That's the kind of stuff you need to practice every day. You need to be like a baseball pitcher and put your shot *exactly* where you want it."

Jacob finally stopped to catch his breath. "You know what the trouble with soccer is," he said. "I just figured it out."

Heidi was smiling. "What?"

"It's too hard. Even when you get good, it's too hard to score. You can play a whole game and you're lucky to get a goal or two."

Heidi bounced the ball off one thigh and then the other in a steady rhythm. "Yeah, that's right. But when you finally *do* score, it feels *sooooo* good. That's why everyone goes so crazy."

Sweat was running down the side of her face, and she was breathing fairly hard, but she kept the ball going.

"I play tennis," Heidi said. "And I run on the track team. And I've played all the other sports." She caught a quick breath. "But I've never been so psyched in any sport as when my team finally gets a goal in soccer."

Jacob motioned for Nate to throw him his ball. Nate did, and Jacob tried to juggle off his thighs the way Heidi was doing. But he couldn't do it very well. He could manage maybe three or four bounces, but then he would hit it wrong, and it would go flying away from him.

"I love to *stop* goals," Nate said. "I have this dream that I'm playing for America the first time we make it to the finals of the World Cup. Some great South American or European team is blasting away at me—and I'm stopping *everything*. And this enormous crowd in one of those gigantic European stadiums is going absolutely wild. They're all chanting my name, and . . ."

Suddenly Nate stopped and laughed at

himself. "Well, you know. It's just a dream," he said. He seemed a little embarrassed.

"Is that really what you want?" Jacob asked. "To play big-league soccer—or whatever it's called?"

"Yup. International."

"Is your family nuts over soccer—the same as you?" Jacob was trying to juggle again. But he was soon running after the ball as it bounced away from him.

"My parents have seen me play maybe three or four times, and I've been playing for four years," Nate said. "They don't have *time* to come more often. That's what they tell me. But they're *important* people, you know."

Jacob wasn't sure what to say. He felt sorry for Nate. He knew that Nate lived in a really fancy house, but he didn't know much about his family.

Jacob looked at Heidi. "I saw your dad at the game," he said. "He was cheering more than anyone. He was really getting into it."

"Yeah," Heidi said. "He's a wild man. He even yells for me at my tennis matches. My mom has to keep telling him to be quiet."

"My mom's the athlete in our family," Jacob said. "She's the one who talked me into playing soccer."

"I knew I liked something about her," Heidi said, and she laughed. "Tell her you have to have a soccer ball. She'll understand."

"I don't want one," Jacob said.

Nate and Heidi both leaned in on Jacob. "You don't *what*?" Heidi said.

"Hey, I just don't want to turn into weirdos like you two. I don't want to start talking to soccer balls or taking them to movies or *anything* like that."

Heidi grinned, and then she said, "You don't *have* to hold it in your arms at night—like Nate," she said. "Just keep it under your kitchen table and feed it table scraps. And maybe let it lick your face once in a while."

"You *are* nuts," Jacob said.

But he was starting to feel at home with Nate and Heidi. He liked them. And they both seemed to believe in him.

"Okay, let's get going," Nate said. "We need to work on your defense. The more times you stop those guys in the middle of the field, the fewer good shots they blast at me."

Heidi told Jacob to mark her while she tried to dribble past him or pass off to Nate. And suddenly she was that other Heidi—intense and focused.

She would feint and change speeds, reverse and turn, and the ball really did seem to be *part* of her. She never looked at it.

Heidi knew all the "cuts," and she used them. She could do a tight 360° turn, keeping herself between Jacob and the ball.

She could also pull the ball back with the sole of her shoe, cut it behind the opposite leg and reverse her direction. Half the time she would leave Jacob standing there when he thought he was about to make a steal.

She had Jacob practice the cuts, but mostly she had him try to stop her. "Watch the ball. Watch the ball," Nate kept yelling, and Jacob found himself improving.

They kept at it for a long time until finally they were both breathing hard, and Heidi was having trouble getting by Jacob.

"All right. Great," Heidi said, and she stopped. She took a couple of gulps of air.

"I told you to play it sort of safe against Jackson. But remember, every now and then you have to gamble and go for the steal."

Jacob shook his head. "It's hard," he said.

Heidi laughed. "That's right. But, boy, does it feel good when you take a ball away from some guy who thinks he's a hot dribbler."

"Yeah, well, according to you two, everything in soccer feels good—when you can finally do it. But what about the way you feel when you *can't* do it?"

"We don't talk about that. That's why we're practicing," Heidi said.

And they kept at it until Jacob's legs felt like rubber. And then they kept at it some more.

★ 5 ★

Tornado Watch

Coach Toscano worked hard with the team for another week, and then he set up another practice game. This time the game was with the Santa Rita Tornadoes—another one of the teams in their league that Angel Park would be playing.

Santa Rita had one of the best teams every year. Nate told Jacob, "You've got to use everything you've learned. These guys are good."

And Jacob found out he was right.

For the first five or six minutes Angel Park played tough defense, and the Tornadoes couldn't get anything going.

But neither could Angel Park. The

Tornadoes had strong defenders and fast midfielders. They marked their opponents every second.

The player covering Jacob was small, shorter than Jacob, but he could really move with or without the ball. His name was Rockwell, but his teammates called him "Rocket." He was a steely-eyed kid who never showed any emotion, but his mouth was always going. He kept telling Jacob how bad he was. And he wasn't afraid to throw an elbow if he got a chance—and he knew the referee wasn't watching.

Jacob thought he had learned a lot by working with Heidi and Nate, but he still made too many mistakes on attack. He tried some of the dribbling moves he had learned, but he still lost the ball too often.

Or he would spot a teammate breaking, and he would pass—just an instant too late— and the defender would get back to the play in time to intercept.

And then one of the Tornado wings made a hard run down the touchline, dribbling. Henry was on him, but the wing pulled up suddenly and centered the ball near the goal.

One of the forwards was Hugh Roberts, who had been the star of the Santa Rita baseball team. He went up for a header, but Brian jumped with him and headed the ball back upfield.

Jacob had turned to see what was happening, and his man broke away from him. Rocket Rockwell controlled Brian's header and then dribbled back toward the goal. Jacob made a dash to get back, but just as he closed in, Rocket lifted a looping pass.

This time Roberts broke away from his defender and got a clear jump at the ball. He turned as he leaped and headed the ball *hard.*

Bam!

It shot past Nate, and the Tornadoes were ahead, 1 to 0.

Nate had stretched out full length and had tried to bat the ball away, but it was a good two feet beyond his reach.

Nate looked really upset with himself. He didn't get up for a time. He slugged the ground hard, and then he just lay there on his chest. When he got up, he kicked at the grass, and Jacob could see that he was talking to himself.

But Jacob knew the goal hadn't happened on that one shot.

It had happened when Jacob let his man get away so that he could bring the ball up for an easy, unguarded pass. And it happened when Roberts broke away and got into the air without anyone there to battle him.

A goal was a team effort. And defense took a whole team too. The coach always talked about playing tough in every part of the field, not just near the goals. Now Jacob understood what he was talking about.

Jacob remembered what Heidi had said. It felt *sooooo* good to get a goal. But it also felt bad—*reeeeeally* bad—to give one up.

He watched the Tornadoes celebrate. The whole team leaped in the air—like they had all been shocked by electricity at the same time—and then they all charged each other.

Roberts took the chance to yell to Sterling, "Hey, Malone, you guys beat us in baseball, but no way are you going to *touch* us in soccer."

Sterling said nothing, and the Angel Park team walked slowly back to their positions, ready for the kickoff. Jacob was breathing hard already.

"Those guys are jerks," Chris said as he walked by Jacob. His dark hair was already dripping with sweat. He wiped his forehead with his sleeve and then brushed his hair back with his fingers.

"Yeah, I know," Jacob said. "They were the same way in baseball."

"Let's get 'em. We can do it," Chris said. But Jacob wasn't sure that Chris really believed they could do it.

Jacob said, "Yeah!" But he didn't believe they could do it either.

He was soon running again. On attack he tried surging, faking, breaking—anything to get clear long enough to take a pass. But he had trouble shaking his defender. Rocket was experienced—and smart. He knew when to cover tight and when to let Jacob overwork himself.

Jacob could see that he could learn from that.

When the Tornadoes kicked the ball across the touchline, the action stopped for a few seconds. Jacob took the chance to take some deep breaths.

"What's the matter, kid? You tired?" Rockwell asked, and he laughed. But he was breathing pretty hard himself.

Jacob had an idea. He sort of gasped but didn't answer. And then he leaned over and took some deep breaths. He wanted Rockwell to think he was dead on his feet.

As Sterling got ready to make the throw-in, Jacob put his hand on his chest as though he were having a hard time breathing. But as he did so, he pointed to the direction he was going to break.

Sterling pulled the ball back over his head, and Jacob suddenly feinted to his right and broke hard to his left.

Sterling threw the ball before Jacob even took off, and he led Jacob perfectly.

Jacob got clear long enough to take the throw, and for once he took the ball in stride and dribbled forward.

Before he could be marked, he passed ahead to Heidi. She made a good run, but she was covered, and when she tried to get a shot off, the defender deflected it. The ball went wide of the goal and across the goal line.

But that meant a corner kick for Angel Park.

Chris took the ball to the corner, and Angel Park set up its play—one they had practiced all week. Clayton and Heidi stayed wide, on either side of the goalposts, and Sterling took up a position in front of the goal area.

Just as Chris kicked the ball—a high center kick—both Clayton and Heidi broke toward the goal. The ball arched in close to the corner, and Clayton tried to head it in.

But the defender leaped into him and knocked him off balance.

Clayton came down screaming, "Foul! Foul!"

But he didn't have to argue. The referee had already made the call.

That meant a penalty shot for Clayton since the foul was in the goal area.

The fullback who committed the foul didn't say much, but Roberts was furious. "He hardly touched him!" he shouted to the referee.

But the referee stepped up to him and said, "You yell like that again and you'll get a yellow card."

Roberts spun around and walked away. Two yellow cards and a guy would be kicked out of the match and then have to miss the next game. No one wanted that to happen—at least not Roberts.

Clayton paid no attention to all that. He was getting ready for his shot. It would be one-on-one—Clayton against the goalie.

The teams moved back outside the goal area, and Clayton took his stance, leaning forward, ready to run toward the ball.

"Okay, drive it home!" Heidi yelled to Clayton, but then everyone quieted down.

Clayton trotted forward.

His eyes were on the bottom right corner, and he angled toward the ball as though he wanted to shoot it that way. The goalie got ready to dive to that side, but Clayton's leg whipped through and drove the ball to the left side.

Goal!

And suddenly Jacob was in the air, yelling and celebrating just the way the Tornadoes had done a few minutes before.

He slammed hands with Clayton and the other players, and then he charged upfield, eager to get going again. Suddenly, he felt strong again. He seemed to have plenty of breath.

"Good work back there, Jacob," Coach Toscano shouted to him. "Good move to get open. Good pass!"

And Jacob knew what the coach meant. Jacob hadn't gotten the goal, but he had helped get Heidi in a good position. That only got them a corner kick, but a corner kick always created possibilities for a goal.

And now the score was tied.

Jacob was starting to see how the whole field mattered, how all the parts had to fit together.

"We can *beat* these guys!" someone yelled.

Jacob spun around. It was Chris he was hearing, but he hardly sounded like the same guy. Chris was starting to believe they could do it.

And so was Jacob.

And he was still feeling that confidence the next time he got the ball.

Nate made a good stop on a long shot, and he rolled the ball out to Jared Trajillo. Jared made a quick pass over to Tammy Hill, and she volleyed the ball upfield.

The pass was intended for Lian, but Tammy hit it too long. Lian chased it, but a defender was blocking his path.

"Get it!" Lian yelled to Jacob.

Jacob ran hard. He got to the ball, made a quick stop, and then cut the ball behind his left leg. He swept the ball forward with the inside of his left foot. He pushed it over to his right foot as he broke upfield.

It was a nice move, and he felt a surge of joy as he realized he had a step on the defender. But a Tornado fullback came up to meet him, and he was suddenly sandwiched by two defenders. He knew he had dribbled too long. He should have passed off.

Lian was yelling again. "Jacob. Jacob. Here!"

But Jacob was trying to fight off the defenders. And suddenly the fullback swept his leg in and kicked the ball away. Another fullback picked it up for the Tornadoes and started his team upfield.

Jacob was stung, knowing that he had let the ball get away. He fell back quickly and marked the nearest player before he realized it wasn't Rockwell but the other midfielder. The fullback passed off to Rockwell, who was wide open.

Jacob was caught for a moment, not sure whether he should charge back to cover his man or cover the one he was on. Rockwell passed off to the other midfielder, and then he took a pass back. Jacob was not tight on either one.

"I've got this guy," Lian yelled, but then the right wing broke to the center. Rockwell hit him with a pass, and the wing drove the ball immediately upfield to Roberts.

Trenton Daynes picked him up, but

Trenton wasn't very fast, and Roberts surprised him with a sudden burst toward the goal. And just as suddenly, he stopped and passed to the left wing coming from the opposite side.

The wing was wide open, and he drove a shot past Brian. Nate dove and knocked the ball away, but he couldn't catch it. The ball rolled in front of the goal, and Roberts charged after it. He took the ball under control, faked to the left, and watched for Nate to commit himself.

And then he *slammed* the ball into the right side of the net.

The Tornadoes were up 2 to 1.

Jacob stamped his foot. He couldn't keep letting this happen. It was his fault the Tornadoes had gotten up the field before his fullbacks could get set.

Jacob walked over to Nate. "Sorry. That was my fault, not yours," he said.

Nate shrugged. He was about to say something when, nearby, Clayton said in that English accent, "At least you know that. That's a start."

Jacob wasn't sure how to take that. If it

was a compliment, it surely wasn't much of one.

He trudged back up the field.

He was feeling tired again.

★ 6 ★

Time to Find Out

"Okay, kids, sit down," Coach Toscano told his team as they walked off the field at half-time. "You looked good out there. I'd say 2 to 1 is not bad. These guys thought they were going to have no trouble with us."

Jacob knew that was true. But he also knew that the Tornadoes had gotten off a lot more shots. They had dominated the middle of the field.

Lian sat down next to Jacob. "I make too many mistakes," he said. "That big guy steals the ball from me almost every time I get it."

"You took it from him a few times, too," Jacob said.

"Not so many times."

And that was true. Lian was *very* quick on

his feet, which sometimes made up for mistakes. But he was having the same problem that Jacob was. Neither one had enough experience against players as good as these Tornado midfielders.

"Players," the coach said, "you're still holding on to the ball too long. A quick pass is better than dribbling. When you dribble the play slows, and not only your defender, but *all* defenders, have a better chance to cover."

"It's hard to find anyone to pass to," Sterling said. "They mark really close."

"I know that. That's why the ball should move, move, move. You have to run to space, and get yourself open. Then, when you get the ball, you have to know where everyone else is and be ready to pass off."

Jacob wondered how he was supposed to do all that. How could he get free, watch the ball as it came to him, and at the same time know where other people were?

Maybe this game wasn't hard. Maybe it was impossible.

But the coach was laughing. "Hey, don't look so down in the mouth. You're playing *ten times* better than last week. If you keep improving that much every week, no one will stop you!"

The coach let the players rest and get a drink, but he came over to Jacob and Lian and kneeled down by them. "Listen, boys, I put you where you are because you are *capable* of being very good. You're getting beat in the middle, but you're getting better. That's what I care about. All right?"

"I can't see everything around me the way you say I should," Jacob said.

"Yes. I can't do that either," Lian said.

The coach nodded and smiled. "I know. A team has to play together, get the feel of how things move and flow." He laughed. "Time. It takes time. But you're getting better. You're both going to be very good."

Jacob had come out of the game for a while in the first half, but now he was going in again. Adam Snarr was coming in for Lian.

Adam had played soccer longer than Lian, but he didn't have Lian's quickness. That meant all the more pressure on Jacob.

And he soon felt it.

The Angel Park team had come together

pretty well at times in the first half. But now they started making mistakes again.

Early in the second half, Brian let the girl who played right forward for the Tornadoes get behind him, and he tried to catch up. He pushed her just before she reached the goal area. The referee called a foul and gave her an indirect free kick.

According to the rules, she couldn't score on the shot until the ball touched someone else. But she was in close.

Angel Park set up their wall—four players lined shoulder to shoulder across her shooting line. Jacob helped form the wall, and he knew that he had to stay tight and keep his hands where they couldn't accidentally touch the ball.

But when the ball hit Jared's legs and bounced away, Jacob didn't respond quickly, and neither did the others.

The left forward got to the ball and fired it right back to the girl who had taken the free kick.

Jacob heard Nate scream, "Cover her! Cover her!"

But it was too late. She was wide open.

Nate came out of the goal and charged

toward her, but he was an instant too late, and she was able to loop the ball over his head. Jacob watched the shot rise, and he thought it would go wide.

But then it bent in the air—like a curve ball—and slipped inside the goalpost.

Jacob knew that players curved their shots by putting spin on the ball. He had even tried it. But he couldn't make it work.

The Tornado forward could!

Now it was 3 to 1.

And Roberts was smarting off again. "Hey, Nate, did someone nail you to the ground? You're a little slow, aren't you?"

The Tornadoes all laughed. Nate didn't say anything.

But Clayton yelled, "Shut your mouth, Roberts."

That didn't go well with Coach Toscano. He called Clayton over and told him he wouldn't put up with any of that.

But Jacob knew that Clayton was still fuming. He was a great player, but he was frustrated. He didn't like to lose. And the losing wasn't *his* fault—at least not in his mind.

Right after the kickoff that followed the score, Angel Park knocked the ball over the touchline. The Tornadoes threw in, and someone left the right wing unmarked. The wing took the ball down the touchline until Brian picked him up. He faked a center pass and then broke into the middle.

The left forward shook loose toward the corner of the goal, just as the wing shot him a hard, low pass.

He took the pass right out of the air with the inside of his foot. He didn't try to power the ball. He just nudged it so it suddenly changed directions.

Nate was right there, but the forward was almost on top of him, and Nate had no time to react. The ball rolled under Nate's arm and into the net.

4 to 1.

Suddenly Angel Park was falling apart.

Jacob walked up the field again. His lungs were screaming. His thighs were burning. He found himself thinking that he should have just stayed with baseball. At least on a baseball diamond he felt as though he could help his team.

Sterling was in front of him, walking with

his hands on his hips. "No one killed us like this in baseball," Jacob said.

Sterling looked around. "Forget about baseball," he said. "We're going to beat these guys some time. We just gotta stop making stupid mistakes."

Jacob wanted to believe that, but right now he would have preferred to face Roberts when the guy was pitching. He'd like to knock a few line drives right past him.

Angel Park kicked off, but before anyone knew what had happened, the Tornadoes had the ball again.

They were on the attack, and Jacob had to mark his man.

But just when he thought he was too tired to run, a Santa Rita player made a bad pass. Jacob shot forward and stole it. Adam saw that Jacob was about to get the ball, and he broke away from his defender.

"Here, here," he shouted in his squeaky voice.

Jacob stroked the ball to him. Adam then dribbled the ball a few yards upfield and shot the ball over to Sterling.

Sterling was marked pretty well, and so he socked the ball right back to Adam.

Jacob had seen what was going to happen, and he burst upfield to a clear space and took a quick pass. Clayton, who hadn't gotten the ball very much today, broke across the center of the field and Jacob kicked the ball to him.

The defense was falling back quickly. Clayton had to strike. He stopped in front of a big fullback, cut the ball with his right foot behind his left, and then broke to the left.

But the defender recovered quickly and stayed close.

When Clayton saw he had no shot, he passed the ball back to Jacob, who was closing in toward the goal area.

Jacob was open, but he only had a split second. The ball skidded across the grass, and Jacob controlled it with the inside of his foot. He then drove a hard, low shot at the corner of the goal.

The goalie, who had seen the shot coming, broke to the corner and dove at the ball.

As the ball passed beyond the goalie's hands and into the net, Jacob couldn't believe it for a moment.

He had done exactly what Heidi had

taught him to do. He had bent forward over the ball, had driven it with the top of his foot—right across the shoelaces—and then landed on that same foot.

He really was learning. He had done it!

He was still just standing there, not sure he believed it, when Heidi almost knocked him down. She jumped on him from the side and sent him spinning. But she was shouting, "Way to go, Jacob! *Way to go!*"

And Clayton was next to get to him. "Great shot!" he screamed. *"Perfect!"*

And Heidi was right. It felt good.

Sooooo good!

As good as a long home run.

But then, Jacob had never really hit a long home run. Maybe his mom was right.

Maybe soccer was Jacob's sport. Suddenly baseball was the farthest thing from his mind.

But just then Clayton said, "I'm afraid it was mostly luck. I doubt he could do it again."

He had spoken to Heidi, but he said it loudly enough for Jacob to hear.

Jacob turned and walked up the field.

Clayton could be a first-class jerk.

But he was probably right.

★ 7 ★

Big Changes

Angel Park lost the game 4 to 2, but they played pretty well after Jacob's goal, and they walked off the field feeling better about themselves.

The following day Coach Toscano held a practice. But after the warmups, he called the team together for a talk. "We're doing much better," he said. "But we aren't getting many chances to score. Other teams are controlling the middle of the field."

Jacob thought he knew what that meant. He wouldn't be starting anymore. But that didn't really surprise him. In a way, he was relieved. At least he wouldn't have to feel so responsible for the team's problems.

"So I've decided to move Clayton to mid-field," the coach said. "He's our strongest, most experienced player, and he can direct the game from there—control the passing and help get the ball up the field."

"But coach!" Clayton said, and then he stopped. He seemed to be at a loss for words.

"I know. You like to play forward."

"I *am* a forward. I'm a *striker*. That's what I've always played."

"I understand that. But for now, the team needs an experienced ball controller in the middle. And we need your defensive skills there too."

"Who'll play *my* position?" Clayton asked. He sounded angry.

"I've thought a lot about that. You saw the shot Jacob made yesterday. He's very quick, and he's catching on to the game. For right now he can maybe help us more at forward than at midfield."

Now Clayton *was* mad. He stood up. "Coach, he just started playing competition soccer. He makes more mistakes than the rest of us put together."

Coach Toscano stepped toward Clayton and put a hand on his shoulder. "Clayton, that's enough of that. I need you to lead the team in the middle. You might get more shots from that position than you've been getting. I think we'll get the ball into shooting range more often."

Jacob watched Clayton. He seemed ready to say he wouldn't do it. But the words didn't come out.

Practice began.

Jacob felt sort of sick. He agreed with Clayton. He wasn't ready to be a forward.

And his lack of confidence soon showed up.

The coach had the team play some five-on-five soccer to get Jacob used to the position. But Jacob struggled. He tried to get clear for passes, but Chris dogged him constantly. When he did get the ball, he couldn't break free to shoot.

Chris stole the ball a number of times, and then when Jacob finally found room to shoot, he was too anxious and drove the ball wide, or he leaned back too much and lofted the ball high. The shot he had taken the day before really did seem to have been nothing but luck.

And all the while Clayton was telling him

what he was doing wrong. "You can't stay in front of the goal all the time. You have to move in and out," he yelled.

But when Jacob moved off to the side and then broke to the goal area, Clayton would scream, "Too late! Too late! You have to see what I'm going to do and get there ahead of the ball!"

Jacob had no idea what that was supposed to mean. How could he know what Clayton was going to do until he did it?

And then, finally, Jacob made his break just as Clayton arched a crossing pass. Jacob wasn't as tall as Clayton, and he was still learning how to head the ball. But Jacob could see that Heidi had no chance for the pass, and so he leaped.

But he mistimed the jump, and the ball grazed off the top of his head and bounced away. It was a beautiful pass, and if Clayton had been receiving it instead of kicking it, he would have knocked the ball home.

Everyone knew it.

Especially Jacob.

Clayton had finally had enough. "This is *stupid*!" he yelled. "How can he play forward when he can't even head the ball?"

Coach Toscano had also had enough. "Come here, Clayton!" he demanded, and he walked away from the other players.

Clayton took his time. Still, he did as he was told.

But then Coach Toscano said, "Jacob, you come here too."

When Jacob came up to them, the coach said, "Clayton, you know better than to act this way. I wish I had two of you—to play forward *and* halfback. But I don't. What I do have is a young man who has athletic ability and not much experience. He'll be a good player, but you have to be patient with him."

Clayton had his hands on his hips, and he was looking down at the grass. "I've *always* been a forward," he mumbled.

"I'm asking you to be more than that. I'm asking you to be my team leader. And that means you have to give Jacob a chance. You can't teach him by shouting at him and making him look bad in front of everyone. You've got to *show* him, and you've got to encourage him."

Clayton wouldn't even look at the coach—or at Jacob.

"Will you do that?" the coach finally asked.

Clayton hesitated for a time, but then he said, "All right. But I—"

"No more 'buts,' Clayton. Will you do it or not?"

Clayton nodded. "Yes."

But he didn't slap Jacob on the back and say, "I'm with you." In fact, he didn't say a word to Jacob during the rest of the practice. He might have stopped making fun of Jacob and yelling at him, but he didn't *teach* him anything.

And that continued all week. Every time Jacob messed up, he would hear Clayton laugh, or he would look up and see Clayton glaring at him.

Jacob got to hate that look. He would almost rather have heard what the guy had to say. Jacob hadn't *asked* for this position. He didn't even want it.

The Angel Park team had only one more practice game before their big preseason tournament. And the game was against a team they had a chance to beat: the Desert Palm Gila Monsters.

But when game day came and the Angel

Park players took the field, Clayton was still avoiding Jacob.

Jacob made up his mind to forget everything else and just concentrate on playing as best he could. If he let the team down, maybe the coach would put someone else in—and that would take the pressure off. And since he knew he would never please Clayton, he figured there was no reason to worry about it.

At least that's what he told himself. But he *did* worry. He just couldn't help it.

Jacob also found that even as a forward he still had to mark a player, and he still had to work the ball for a shot. In that sense, the position was not so different from midfield.

But . . . there was one *big* difference.

Once the ball got into scoring position, he felt a lot more responsibility. What he wanted was for Clayton and Heidi to handle the attack. But he knew he couldn't stand back. He had to get free and take passes. And he may have to shoot.

It didn't take long to see, however, that Clayton was thinking much the same way.

He worked the ball through midfield better than Jacob ever had. He was a much better dribbler, but he also passed sharply and then got free to get the ball back.

But once he got into shooting range, he stayed away from Jacob. He would either drive the ball on the dribble and try to get off his own shot, or he would look for a pass to Heidi or one of the wings.

A couple of times Jacob burst into open space and was ready for a pass, and Clayton simply took the ball in the opposite direction.

Coach Toscano kept yelling to Clayton to watch Jacob, but Clayton didn't listen.

Still, Angel Park was keeping the pressure on. They were winning the battle in the middle of the field, and they had possession of the ball most of the time.

Clayton and Heidi both got off shots, but the Desert Palm goalie made good saves. Sterling had a great chance on a rebound off a fullback's legs, but his shot went wide.

Nate made some good stops of his own for Angel Park, and the half kept ticking away without anyone scoring.

And then, as time was running out, Clayton made an all-out push. He took a pass from Lian and rushed past his defender. He charged down the field, and a fullback came up to meet him. The guy who had been defending Jacob also broke toward Clayton.

Clayton was doubled, and Jacob was wide open. Jacob was scared, but he still yelled, "Clayton! Clayton!" But Clayton tried to split the defenders and dribble between them.

One of the fullbacks stepped in for a tackle, and the other closed in tight. In the struggle the ball popped loose, and Heidi dashed over and took control. She instantly shot a hard pass to Jacob.

Jacob saw his chance for a clear shot. But when he reached out to control the pass, he hit it too hard with the inside of his foot. The ball bounced back, and he had to chase after it. By then defenders were closing in. He hurried to get off a shot, but he rushed too much, and he didn't really hit it solid.

The ball bounded toward the goal, but the goalie had plenty of time to run over and scoop it up.

The goalie ran free and then punted the ball far upfield. A few seconds later the half ended, and the score remained 0 to 0.

Jacob heard what Clayton said as the team walked off the field. "Some shot that was. This guy is supposed to be a forward?"

Jacob had to agree. He hoped the coach would take him out of the game for the second half. In fact, Jacob was even thinking that he might quit soccer. Playing forward wasn't worth the kind of pressure he was feeling.

As he walked off the field, he saw his friends from baseball and from school, Kenny Sandoval and Harlan Sloan. They were standing on the sidelines.

"Jacob," Harlan shouted. "Way to go. You're looking good."

Jacob stopped and shook his head. "I messed up that shot," he said. "I should have had the goal."

"Hey, that stuff happens," Kenny said. "Don't worry about it. You're playing great."

Jacob thought back to baseball and the way his friends always yelled for him when he walked up to bat. He could have used some of that right now. He really wished it was still baseball season.

He'd rather try his luck with a bat any day.

★ 8 ★

Hope

The coach didn't have a lot to say at half-time, but he made his words count. "Clayton," he said, "you're trying to do too much yourself, and the defense is collapsing on you. You have to trust your forwards."

He didn't say *both* forwards. But everyone knew what he meant.

Nate came over and sat down by Jacob. "Just keep getting open, and he'll have to pass to you," he said. "Or someone will. Your defender is cheating off you to cover Clayton, and that means you're going to get your chance."

"I'd rather just let someone else give it a try."

"Just don't get too jumpy when you get a chance to shoot. Sometimes that split second to line up the shot is more important than hurrying too much."

That was all well and good, but Jacob still felt awkward and unnatural with the ball. He wished he could pick it up and toss it at the goal.

Just before the team went back on the field, Coach Toscano came over to Jacob and said, "You're still fighting the ball. You have to relax and be loose. When your body is tight, you can't flow, and the ball bounces off you like a wall."

That was probably true, but Jacob wondered how he could relax with all this pressure on him.

"Remember. You and the ball have to be *one*. It's not your enemy. It's part of you."

"Yeah, right," Jacob thought, "and I ought to kiss it good night, the way Nate does," but he didn't say it. He trotted onto the field.

Kenny and Harlan were yelling for him. So were his parents. In fact, a lot of the parents were there today. It was the biggest crowd they had had all season. But that didn't make things any easier.

With no score so far, the game might come down to one goal.

Or one big mistake.

The first time Jacob got control of the ball in the second half, he made a good steal. The Desert Palm sweeper was trying to clear the ball to the goalie. Jacob started upfield and then doubled back quickly and took the sweeper by surprise.

He raced in and trapped the ball, and then tried to get a shot off before anyone could cover him.

But he kicked frantically, hit the ball too much with his toe, and shot the ball high over the goal.

"I can't believe it!" he heard Clayton say. "He finally does something right, and then he blows a shot like that!"

But Heidi told him, "Good steal, Jacob. Just relax more when you shoot."

Jacob had heard that advice somewhere before.

The second half, however, soon took on

the same pattern as the first half. Clayton dominated the middle of the field, and he, Lian, Chris, and Henry kept getting the ball into shooting range.

Clayton seemed to feel he had to take the shot himself, and he kept working to get free.

Two defenders were usually chasing him, and when he looked to pass, he always looked to Heidi. But she was well marked, too, and neither of them could get off an open shot.

But Lian could see what was happening.

A couple of times he tried to get the ball to Jacob, who was getting free. But the two couldn't seem to connect with any timing. Either the pass was late, or Jacob would have trouble controlling the ball before someone would cover him.

Gradually, the Gila Monsters were having better luck getting the ball forward, but the Angel Park backs were doing a great job shutting down any direct shots. And Nate was blocking anything that did get past them.

The score was still 0 to 0, and the thirty-minute half was running along fast.

And then Clayton took a throw-in from

the touchline and hit Henry with a good pass. Henry took the ball down the side. Clayton trailed, and then he broke to the center, and Henry crossed to him.

The pass was a little long, however, and a Desert Palm fullback controlled it and tried to clear it back upfield.

But Clayton reacted quickly and darted back to the ball, cutting off the Desert Palm wing. He did a quick reverse cut and shook a defender who turned the wrong way.

Suddenly he was driving toward the goal. But the sweeper was coming up fast.

"Clayton!" Jacob yelled, and he broke to the goal.

Clayton seemed to react before he could think. He shot a quick pass to Jacob, slowed for a second, and then charged hard past his defender.

Jacob saw the break and remembered what they had practiced all week.

He kicked the ball behind the sweeper, just as Clayton broke past him. It was the old give-and-go play—what soccer players called a "wall pass"—and it worked to perfection.

The pass had come before Clayton broke,

so there was no offside, but suddenly now Clayton had clear sailing to the goal. He slowed a little and ran forward under control. Before the goalie could come out on him, he faked to the left and then fired the ball with his left foot into the right side of the goal.

The goalie dove, but his reaction had been an instant too slow.

Score!

Clayton leaped in the air and shouted, "All right!" And he had hardly landed before he spun and looked at Jacob. "Great pass," he shouted. His voice gave away how surprised he was.

But Jacob was just as surprised. They had practiced the wall pass plenty, but at the moment, things had happened so quickly that Jacob acted without thinking.

It was almost as though he and Clayton had been two parts of one motion. Something natural. Something like the coach was always talking about—being one.

The Angel Park players all charged to the goal and grabbed Clayton. But then they surrounded Jacob, slapped him on the back, and yelled their congratulations.

"Jacob," Heidi shouted above the rest. "That was it! Just what we've been practicing."

Jacob liked that.

Over on the sidelines, Kenny and Harlan were screaming as though they were on the team themselves. And Jacob's mom was cheering louder than anyone.

Then disaster struck.

After the kickoff, the Gila Monsters took the ball up the field, and the right forward somehow got loose on a breakaway. Billy tried a desperate sliding tackle, but he knocked the forward's legs out from under him.

Tripping.

In the goal area.

That meant a penalty shot, and the forward made a great shot past Nate.

And so, just like that, the score was tied again.

And time was running down.

Their first win had been in their pockets, and now they were probably going to have to settle for a tie.

But Clayton was intense about saving the day. Soon after the kickoff, he took a long pass from Nate and started upfield, dribbling. As a defender marked him, he kicked a quick pass to Lian, who broke forward a little and then heeled the ball back to Clayton.

Jacob saw that the two were starting to have more of a sense of where the other was going to be.

But this was it. Time was running out, and they wouldn't get many more chances.

Clayton took the ball to the left wing, dropped it off for Chris, and then took a quick return pass. Chris looped around his defender, and Clayton hit him for a move upfield. But Chris was met by a fullback, and he dropped the ball back to Clayton.

This time Clayton burst down the middle, dribbling.

Jacob thought he was going to go all the way, but defenders pulled in on him, and that's when Clayton stopped suddenly, controlled the ball, and faked a pass to Heidi.

Jacob thought he knew what was coming, and he broke on an angle toward the goal.

Clayton looped a pass into the air, and Jacob went up for it. He couldn't head it. It wasn't high enough. But he cradled it with his chest, bending inward, forming a pocket—like a baseball glove. The ball dropped right to his feet.

He used the sole of his shoe to trap the ball, and then he wheeled to shoot.

But the goalie saw Jacob's angle and was heading toward him to cut off the shot.

Jacob took that split second, pulled back a little, then broke to the right and changed his angle.

Then he lashed his right leg through, keeping his weight over the ball. He slammed the ball exactly where the goalie had been before he made his break.

Goal! Goal! Goal!

Suddenly someone had him around the waist, hoisting him in the air. The voice was muffled because the guy's face was pushed against his middle, but the English accent was easy to recognize.

"You're a forward, you are. You really are a forward!"

But when Jacob's feet hit the ground, he said, "You did it, Clayton. You got it to me!"

Clayton beamed.

And then the whole team came flying in. "We've got 'em now. Just play defense!" Sterling was yelling.

And the team picked up the chant. "Defense! Defense! Defense!"

They ran downfield for the kickoff, and there was no way they were going to lose this one now.

The Gila Monsters played furiously, but Angel Park stacked their defense and cleared the ball every chance they could.

And then suddenly, it was over.

Jacob dropped straight to the ground. He was sure he was too tired to walk off the field. But in a few seconds he was up congratulating his teammates—and the Desert Palm players.

After the hand-slapping and the celebrating were all over, Coach Toscano called the players together. "Now I'm seeing something happen out there," he told them. "I'm seeing some flow. And Jacob, you didn't fight the ball that last time."

Jacob wasn't so sure about that. But at least he hadn't panicked, and something about the play did seem right.

"What about a name?" Coach Toscano finally asked. "Next week we play a tournament. I have to tell the league what our name is."

Nate raised his hand. "I've been thinking about that," he said. "A bunch of lions hunting together is called a 'pride of lions.' They're strong and quick. And you're always saying we should have pride in ourselves. So I was thinking we could be the Angel Park Pride, and it would have both meanings."

Everyone liked the idea.

The Pride was born. And Jacob could feel it.

When he walked off the field his "fans" were waiting. Kenny and Harlan gave him one of their patented three-way high-fives. And then Heidi and Nate came over, and they gave the leaping high-five a try of their own.

And his mom had a box for Jacob, all wrapped up like a birthday present.

Jacob tore off the paper and found just what he wanted.

A soccer ball.

He gave it a great big kiss.

Angel Park Soccer Strategies

Soccer, like football and basketball, is a game of game plans, of strategies. Both professionals and amateurs use strategies to give themselves a general sense of what to do *as a team*. Without teamwork and strategy, soccer games would only be a bunch of people running around a field, kicking a ball back and forth.

This is why players have particular jobs to do, either scoring goals or defending against goals. This makes the game more interesting— and more challenging. When a player is running upfield with the ball, he will almost always be cut off before he scores a goal himself. This is why players learn strategies. When the time comes, they'll know what to do. They'll know where their teammates are without even looking.

Or at least that's the idea. The success of the strategies depends on the skill of the players. The strategies we've presented here, in these diagrams, are standard game plans that the Angel Park Pride might attempt to use in a game. If you think your team could profit from a little strategic thinking, show these to your coach. Give them a try. Good luck!

Kickoff

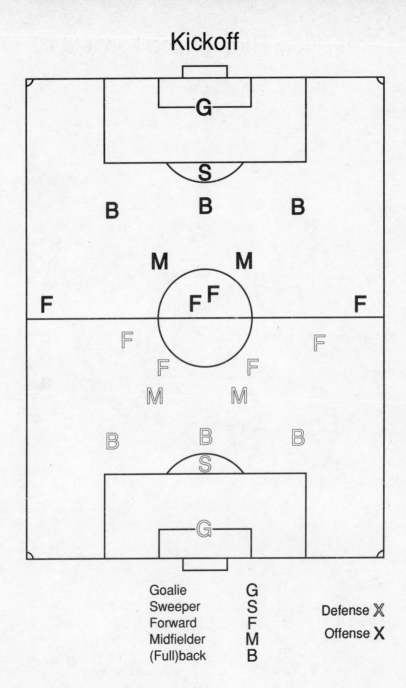

Goalie	G
Sweeper	S
Forward	F
Midfielder	M
(Full)back	B

Defense X

Offense X

95

Transition Through the Midfield #1

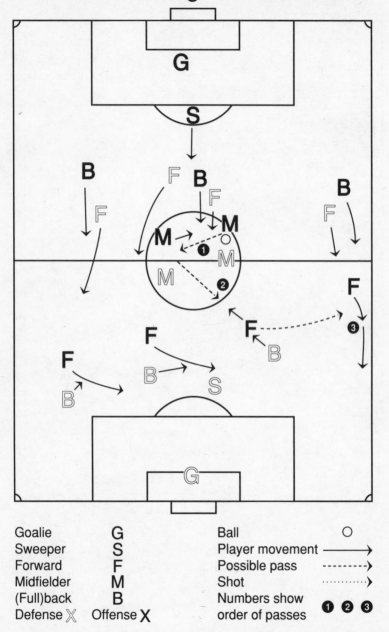

Goalie	G	Ball ○
Sweeper	S	Player movement ⟶
Forward	F	Possible pass ------>
Midfielder	M	Shot ·········>
(Full)back	B	Numbers show ❶ ❷ ❸
Defense X	Offense X	order of passes

Transition Through the Midfield #2

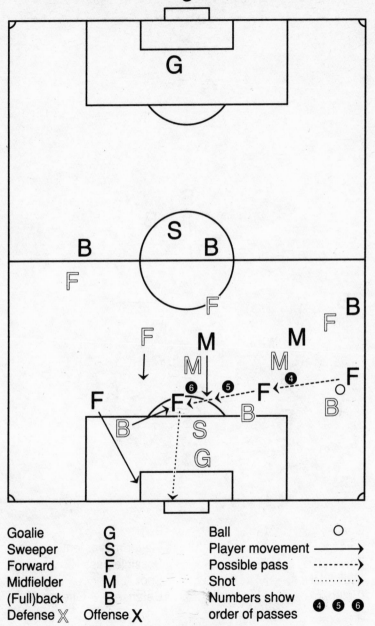

Goalie	G	Ball	○
Sweeper	S	Player movement	⟶
Forward	F	Possible pass	----‣
Midfielder	M	Shot	······‣
(Full)back	B	Numbers show	❹ ❺ ❻
Defense X	Offense X	order of passes	

Defensive Transition to Offense

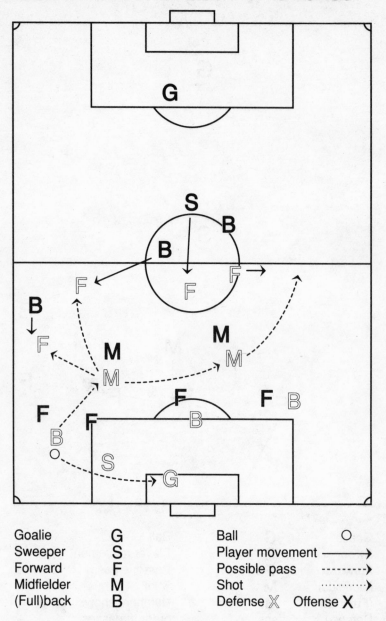

Goalie	G	Ball		O
Sweeper	S	Player movement		——→
Forward	F	Possible pass		----→
Midfielder	M	Shot		·····→
(Full)back	B	Defense X	Offense X	

Offensive Attack on Wing

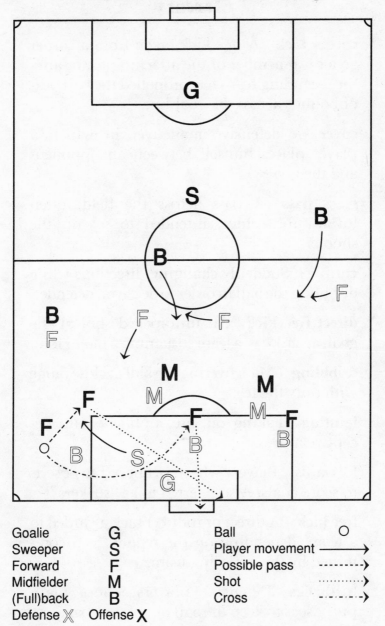

Goalie	G	Ball	O
Sweeper	S	Player movement	⟶
Forward	F	Possible pass	------⟶
Midfielder	M	Shot	·······⟶
(Full)back	B	Cross	·—·—·⟶
Defense X	Offense X		

Glossary

corner kick A free kick taken from a corner area by a member of the attacking team, after the defending team has propelled the ball out-of-bounds across the goal line.

cover A defensive maneuver in which a player places himself between an opponent and the goal.

cross pass A pass across the field, often toward the center, intended to set up the shooter.

cutting Suddenly changing directions while dribbling the ball in order to deceive a defender.

direct free kick An unimpeded shot at the goal, awarded to a team sustaining a major foul.

dribbling Maneuvering the ball at close range with only the feet.

feinting Faking out an opponent with deceptive moves.

forwards Players whose primary purpose is to score goals. Also referred to as "strikers."

free kick A direct *or* indirect kick awarded to a team, depending on the type of foul committed by the opposing team.

fullbacks Defensive players whose main purpose is to keep the ball out of the goal area.

goalkeeper The ultimate defender against attacks on the goal, and the only player allowed to use his hands.

halfbacks See Midfielders.

heading Propelling the ball with the head, especially the forehead.

indirect free kick A shot at the goal involving at least two players, awarded to a team sustaining a minor foul.

juggling A drill using the thighs, feet, ankles, or head to keep the ball in the air continuously.

kickoff A center place kick which starts the action at the beginning of both the first and second halves or after a goal has been scored.

marking Guarding a particular opponent.

midfielders Players whose main purpose is to get the ball from the defensive players to the forwards. Also called "halfbacks."

penalty kick A direct free kick awarded to a member of the attacking team from a spot 12 yards in front of the goal. All other players must stay outside the penalty area except for the goalie, who must remain stationary until the ball is in play.

punt   A drop kick made by the goalkeeper.

shooting   Making an attempt to score a goal.

strikers   See Forwards.

sweeper   The last player, besides the goal-keeper, to defend the goal against attack.

tackling   Stealing the ball from an opponent by using the feet or a shoulder charge.

total soccer   A system by which players are constantly shifting positions as the team shifts from offense to defense. Also called "position-less soccer."

volley kick   A kick made while the ball is still in the air.

wall   A defensive barrier of players who stand in front of the goal area to aid the goalkeeper against free kicks.

wall pass   This play involves a short pass from one teammate to another, followed by a return pass to the first player as he runs past the defender. Also called the "give-and-go."

wingbacks   Outside fullbacks.

wingers   Outside forwards.

DEAN HUGHES has written many books for children, including the popular *Nutty* stories and *Jelly's Circus*. He has also published such works of literary fiction for young adults as the highly acclaimed *Family Pose*. Writing keeps Mr. Hughes very busy, but he does find time to run and play golf— and he loves to watch almost all sports. His home is in Utah. He and his wife have three children, all in college.

It's going to take teamwork...

ANGEL PARK SOCCER STARS #2

Defense!
by Dean Hughes

The preseason soccer tournament is starting, and it's time for the Angel Park Pride to find out what they're made of. Their coach keeps telling them to have fun, but Nate Matheson, the team's goalie, takes it a bit more seriously. So when he sees his teammates making dumb mistakes, he loses his temper. But he soon realizes that the only way the team is going to win any games is if he stops yelling and starts leading. The only question is, how can Nate get his teammates to listen if they're all mad at him?

FIRST TIME IN PRINT!

A BULLSEYE BOOK PUBLISHED BY ALFRED A. KNOPF, INC.

Play ball with the kids from Angel Park!

ANGEL PARK ALL-STARS™

by Dean Hughes

Meet Kenny, Harlan, and Jacob—three talented young players on Angel Park's Little League team. They're in for plenty of fastball action...as well as fun and friendship. Collect them all! Watch for new titles and new sports coming soon!

 - ✂